THE MAN IN THE MOON

Elizabeth Edwoods

AuthorHouse™
1663 Liberty Drive
Bloomington, IN 47403
www.authorhouse.com
Phone: 1-800-839-8640

Published by AuthorHouse: 12/19/2014

ISBN: 978-1-4969-3774-2 (sc)
ISBN: 9781496961112 (hc)
ISBN: 978-1-4969-3775-9 (e)

authorHOUSE®

To
my darling daughter
TAMYRA
this book
is
LOVINGLY DEDICATED
and her enduring love for children.

Listen little children,

I am coming down to see

Why you have stopped believing in me.

I am the man in the MOON, I am for real.

Just you wait and I will show

All the things you need to know.

I can do anything you can do.

I can! I can too!

i can RUN

i can JUMP.

I can S K I P

I can H O P

I can even climb a tree to the TOP.

"Can you climb up the hill
like Jack and Jill?"

I can,
I WILL --I WILL!

I can skate on a board. Even skate up a wall,

Then come down again without a fall.

Let's take a SWING up in the air.

Come DOWN and play
turtle and the hare.

FINISH

Come watch me dive and swim.

I can even ride a bike,

We can play hide and seek

Then go for a hike.

I can ski on snow, skate on ice.

Even go around the rink once or twice.

We can play leap frog,
jump UP and
DOWN,

All children love to B^OU N C^E around.

I will fly you to the MOON.

You will see my home SOON.

It's as real as can be,

just the MOON and me.

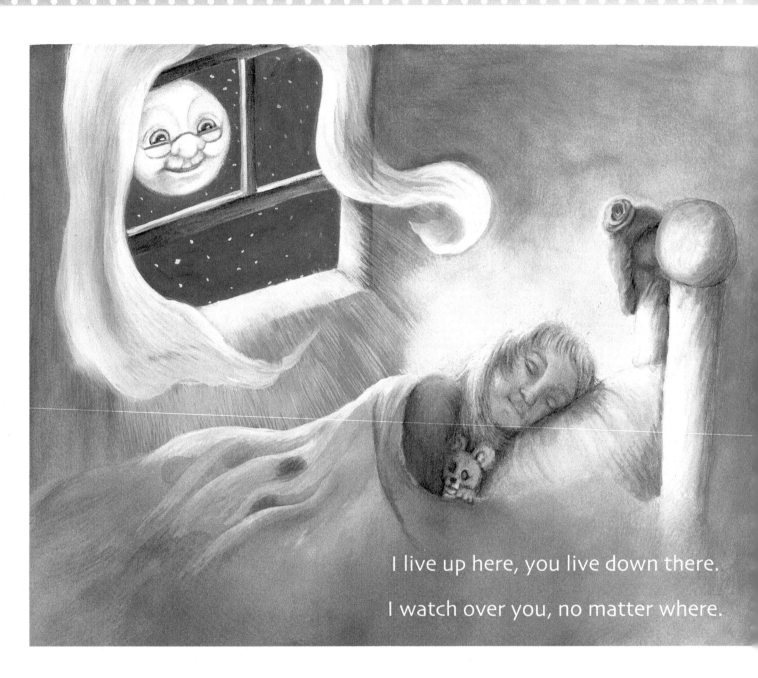

I live up here, you live down there.

I watch over you, no matter where.

When someone says -- there is no man in the moon

Just close your eyes and believe in me.

Then open them again, and you will see.

I am the man in the MOON

I'll be back again SOON. Very SOON.

Now you have seen all I can do

But I can't look down and

forget about YOU.

Tabitha Benedict Aaron was born in upstate New York

where she discovered early on her ability to draw.

Throughout her childhood she filled

a scrapbook with many artistic awards and recognitions.

She currently lives and works in Colorado

where she pursues fine art and illustration full time.

Please visit her at www.tabzartstudio.com

Elizabeth Edwoods Bio

Elizabeth Edwoods was born in Sumter, South Carolina. At the age of five the family moved up North. The first stop was New York City. At the age of twelve she moved to Philadelphia, the city of brotherly love, and it is there she has remained.

She married and was blessed with two daughters, three grandchildren and three great grandchildren. Her love of children and a vivid imagination allowed her to see into a child's world. Elizabeth enrolled in a class for creative writing. This is not her first manuscript, but it is her first book. There are more writings to come.

CPSIA information can be obtained
at www.ICGtesting.com
Printed in the USA
LVOW05*0034240516
489645LV00023B/95/P